SQUID

THE MAGNIFICENT

story by Lynne Berry

pictures by Luke LaMarca

Disney • HYPERION   Los Angeles   New York

KID

I am Squid Kid the Magnificent—
Master of Illusion!
My feats will astound.
My feats will confound.
My deeds will
daze and amaze!

Watch closely.

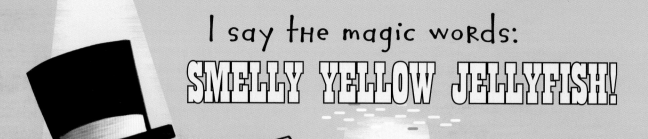

I say the magic words:
SMELLY YELLOW JELLYFISH!

I wave.

I wink.

WINK

I vanish in ink.

Good-bye!

Ignore my sister. I am not Oliver—I am

SQUID KID
THE MAGNIFICENT,

and I am ready for my next trick.

I say

the magic words:

SMELLY

YELLOW

JELLYFISH!

I wave my magic wand.

Dozens and dozens of octopus cousins!

Oliver. Your octopus chums were CAMOUFLAGED.
You know that is NOT magic.

I Repeat: Ignore my sister.

I am not Oliver—

I am SQUID KID THE MAGNIFICENT

and the show must go on.

Watch closely.
Do you see?

In this hand:
a single
ordinary
cuttlefish.

Hey!
My Cuddles!
How is SHE here?
Have you been in
my ROOM?

A good magician
never reveals his secrets.
Now: watch closely.

Trust me.
I am watching you like an eel.

Then you see:
in this hand,
my magic hat.

The cuttlefish is pink.
The hat is empty.

I place the cuttlefish
in the hat.

I say the magic words:

SMELLY YELLOW JELLYFISH!

I tap the hat.

I tip the hat.

Look! And behold:
the cuttlefish
has turned to GOLD!

Cute, Oliver, very cute.
But you KNOW that is not magic.
Cuttlefish change colors
ALL THE TIME.

CUTE, you say?

CUTE?

Ha!

I am . . .

SQUID KID
THE MAGNIFICENT.

You may doubt. You may jeer.
But watch—I am ready for my ultimate feat!
You will shout! You will cheer!
Come forth! Come forth!
I need a volunteer.

Okay, okay.
No need to get
all worked up..

I ask the volunteer
to close her eyes.
I ask the volunteer
to clear her mind.

Tee-Hee.

Look tHeRe,

look HeRe.

No volunteeR.

I made
my sister
disappear.

Ta . . .

. . . da?

Very clever,
Squid Kid,
very clever.

Why thank you, Stella.
I will now take a bow.

But I
am not
Stella.
I am . . .

Tentacula of the Deep—
with eight, great, tanglesome, ticklesome tentacles.

WINK

Always and again: for John —LB

For Teresa, Lynn, and Kevin —LL

Printed in Malaysia
First Hardcover Edition, June 2015
1 3 5 7 9 10 8 6 4 2
H106-9333-5-15146

Library of Congress Cataloging-in-Publication Data

Berry, Lynne.
Squid Kid the Magnificent / by Lynne Berry ; illustrated by Luke LaMarca.—1st ed.
p. cm.
Summary: When Oliver the squid transforms himself into Squid Kid the Magnificent, Master of Illusion,
his older sister Stella is not impressed.
ISBN 978-1-4231-6119-6
[1. Magic tricks—Fiction. 2. Brothers and sisters—Fiction. 3. Squids—Fiction.] I. LaMarca, Luke, ill. II. Title.
PZ7.B461752Squ 2013
[E]—dc23   2011027769

Designed by Joann Hill
Text is set in 24-point Pocket Bold and Sugarplum Sweet

Reinforced binding
Visit www.DisneyBooks.com